I0451180

BACK PORCH SECRETS

Tanya Hilson

Contents

CHAPTER ONE

"Boy, I smell money, and it's the first of the month, time to get paid!" Bobby's phone rang. He pulled it from his pocket, looked at it, then held it to his ear. "What up, Roscoe, you back in town?"

"What's good, Bob? Nah, not yet. I'm on my way, though, and wanted to see if you had some of that Good-Good,".

"You know I keeps the smoke," he answered.

"Okay, hold me down a half-ounce".

"Yup, got you. Make sure you got my half-ounce money."

Debbie, a woman in her early 40s, and Roscoe's girlfriend stepped out onto the porch wearing a pink bath rub with furry pink house shoes. "Hey, Bobby! Surprise to see you up this early."

"Early bird gets the worm. I just talked to Roscoe."

"Yeah? He'll be back on his way after he finishes his loads. I guess he's calling you for something to smoke, huh?". Now, Ms. Debbie, you ear hustling!

"Nah, I just know my man and know what he wants,". She laughed and retreated into her apartment as Ms. Ruby stepped out onto her porch with her bible in hand taking a seat in the chair on her porch.

"Hi, Ms. Ruby! "Mmm-hmm. Hi, Bobby, you sure up early, for someone with no job".

"Old Lady--I mean Ms. Ruby, I do have a job, a job getting these bags." Bobby pulled money out of his pocket as he sat on the stairs counting it.

"Well, you can't put "street pharmacist" on a tax return, or a resume."

"The streets are my job."

Ms. Ruby waved him away, then turned toward her screen door. "Scooter! Get out here and take this garbage down."

A voice came from inside the apartment. "I will, Grandma. Let me finish getting dressed for school, and then I'll take it down.

Ms. Ruby grabbed a broom sitting in the corner of her porch and began sweeping.

Willie, Vicky's husband, a grocery store butcher, stepped out onto his top-floor porch with a cup of coffee in his hand looking down at Ms. Ruby. "Morning, Ms. Ruby! Will I be seeing you at the store today? We got some fresh produce coming in – you know, them collard greens and mustard greens you like. Oh, and we have a sale on some meat packages, too."

"Willie, you are speaking my language child, Food. Well, your wife Vicky is taking me to cash my Social Security check first, then we're going to pick up my medicine, and after that, we'll be heading your way. Plus, I need to play my lottery there too. Is she up yet?"

"Yes, Ma'am. She's in the shower now, Ms. Ruby.

"Okay, you tell her I'm about to make some vittles for my grandson, and then I'll be getting dressed. I should be ready by the time she is." "I'll do just that, Ms. Ruby." Willie stepped back into his apartment. Ms. Ruby finished sweeping her porch, then went inside.

Janice, a caramel complexion young lady in her early 20'S and Bobby's baby mommy walked out onto their porch and placed Bobby Jr. in the playpen. He cried and jumped up and down as she blew on the hot oatmeal to cool it before feeding it to him.

"What's wrong with him?" Bobby asked.

"I guess I'm not feeding him fast enough. He's greedy, just like his daddy." Janice said.

"Whatever! Just feed my son so that he can have muscles, like his daddy." Bobby flexed his biceps, and Janice rolled her eyes.

You think you're all that.

"You know I'm all that, that's why you be getting mad when other women look at me."

"You all right! You, not no Denzel Washington."

Bobby turned to her, instantly enraged, he walked over to Janice and grabbed her hair with a painfully tight grip. "What did you say?" Janice struggled as Bobby pulled her hair.

"I didn't say anything, Bobby!"

2

Bobby stared at Janice with a sinister frown on his face, then released his grip on her hair.

"I thought so! Take your ass in the house, and finish feeding my son."

Janice grabbed the baby and the oatmeal and rushed into the apartment.

Bobby walked up to the screen door behind her.

"And clean this damn house up, too." He attempted to slam the screen door, but it didn't close. "And, get the landlord over here to fix this raggedy-ass door!"

Scooter, Ms. Ruby's teenage grandson, the high school star quarterback, walked out onto the porch with the trash and his backpack standing 6ft tall weighing 200 pounds with a short haircut. "Hey, Bobby, everything good?"

"Yeah, man! We good, Mr. Football Star. Just sometimes, women say dumb shit. Just let anything flow out their mouth. A man like me must set them straight. You know, remind them who's in charge."

Scooter picked up bags of trash from his porch and threw them over the railing into the dumpster. "Nah, I guess we're different because I was taught to treat women with respect. That there is not how I was bought up to treat women."

"I'll give a motherfucker respect when respect is due. Now, if you're grandma sees you throwing garbage over that banister, she's going to snap." Bobby pulled a blunt from behind his ear and lit it up. He took a puff, then try to pass it to Scooter. "You want to hit this?"

"Nah, man! Coach gives us random drug tests. Plus, I got scouts coming out to see me. I'm trying to get this scholarship; I can't be sitting on the bench over no weed."

"Okay, you're right. Get that scholarship, son! Then you can come smoke with Big Bobby."

"Oh, I'm going to get that scholarship, but I'm good on smoking; that's just not me. Weed not my thing, but my future is." Scooter picked up his backpack, stepped down off the porch, and exited through the back gate.

Bobby took a seat on his porch, scrolling through his phone display.

Vicky, Willie's wife in her mid-30s and Ms. Ruby's caregiver stepped out onto her porch wearing a Pink jumpsuit from Victory Secrets, with white Air Force One's, brushing her long black Brazilian wavy hair. She called down to Ms. Ruby's apartment.

"Hey, Ms. Ruby, I'll be coming down in a minute, you ready?"

Ms. Ruby stepped out of her screen door with a cup of coffee in her hand. Gospel Music could be heard faintly from inside her apartment. "What, child? I heard you call my name, but I had my music up." Ms. Ruby pulled the remote to the radio from her jacket pocket, turning the music down.

"I'll be going to the car in a minute; I just need to put my hair in a ponytail, you ready?" Vicky said.

"Child, I've been ready. I'm just sipping on my coffee, listening to my music, waiting for you."

Debbie stepped onto her porch and called down to Ms. Ruby. "Ms. Ruby! I thought I heard you!"

"Hey, Debbie! I'm surprised you're up early, after all, that partying and drinking you did last night."

Debbie stretched to the sky, "Oh, Ms. Ruby, stop! We were just enjoying some cards in this beautiful weather."

"Mm-hmm! It looks like you all were getting drunk to me. Cussing and talking all loud, waking me up out of my sleep."

"Sorry, Ms. Ruby. Roscoe's been on the road. You know I get lonely when he's gone. We'll keep it down next time."

"Mm-hmm! Y'all better, before I have to boil some grits and go old school - Lord, let me hold my tongue."

Debbie lit a cigarette and took a big puff, "Okay, Ms. Ruby, don't nobody need no burnt skin around here."

Debbie's phone rang. She looked at it, then answered, "Hey Roscoe, Ms. Ruby and I were just talking about you."

"Yeah, and what you talking about, how much you been missing big daddy?"

"You know I miss you, baby. So, I see you called Bobby before you called me!"

"Baby, I been driving, I just need some weed to smoke when I get home."

Debbie laughed, "And you better get enough for the both of us, too!" Debbie walked back into her apartment, as Janice stepped out onto her porch holding Bobby Jr."

"Hey Bobby, I need to take Bobby Jr. to his doctor's appointment. Can you give me some money for a cab?" Janice said.

A cab? you better get your ass on that bus. Bobby, you know the bus takes too long, and it's always crowded."

"Do you have cab money, Janice?" Janice sighed, "No."

"Then you better get that damn bus card off the dresser and get to walking to the bus stop."

Hours had passed, and it was late in the afternoon. Debbie was grilling on her porch as Ms. Ruby and Vicky returned from their day of running errands. Vicky carried the bags as they climbed the stairs to Ms. Ruby's porch.

"Child, it seems like we been gone all day," Ms. Ruby said.

"I blame that slow butt pharmacist, but it smells good back here. Looks like Debbie pulled out her grill again. She knows she loves to cook," Vicky said.

Debbie looked over the banister at the two women as she opened a bottle of vodka pouring herself a shot.

"Hey there, Ms. Ruby, Vicky! I see y'all back. Ms. Ruby, did you bring me back anything?" Debbie said.

"No, Debbie, we didn't buy any liquor," Ms. Ruby said. Vicky giggled as she swatted Ms. Ruby on the arm playfully.

"Debbie, you sure got it smelling good up there! What are you cooking?" Vicky asked.

"I got some hot links and burgers going now, and I got some chicken quarters to go on once those come off. I got friends coming over, they then got them checks, so it's time for me to take their money." Debbie returned to the grill as Ms. Ruby and Vicky approached Ms. Ruby's back door. Ms. Ruby whispered to Vicky.

"You notice, she always has company when Roscoe's gone?" Ms. Ruby said.

"Now, Ms. Ruby, be nice. Hell, Roscoe is always gone, so I take it she gets lonely." Vicky said.

"I'm just saying, that child has a party every week."

Vicky took the bags inside as Ms. Ruby settled into one of the chairs on her porch. Vicky returned to the porch and took a seat next to Ms. Ruby.

"I see Scooter hasn't been home yet, his practice must be running late?" Vicky asked.

"Yeah, he's been staying after school putting in extra practice. He says scouts have been coming to see him play. His coach says he's got a good chance to get a scholarship to play college ball," Ms. Ruby said.

"Ms. Ruby, you have sure raised that boy right since his mother passed."

"We take care of each other, Vicky. It wasn't easy: me losing my daughter and scooter losing his mother to a drunk driver. I'm just glad we have each other; he's all I got." Ms. Ruby smiled as she shook her head, rubbing her knee. "We got each other; I just wish I could do more for him."

"You do love you some pork chops."

"I'm going to have a nice garden, where I can just sit back, plant my veggies, and not have to worry about hearing gunshots or getting robbed,"

"I hear you on that, Ms. Ruby. I can't see me and Willie on no farm, though. I want me a big house in the 'burbs, where the rich and famous live you know, like Oprah and Stedman." Vicky said.

"In that case, Willie better keep playing the lottery," Ms. Ruby said. "Oh, you got jokes, Ms. Ruby. I'm going to tighten your kitchen up and wash them little dishes." Vicky went inside Ms. Ruby's apartment as Ms. Ruby followed behind her.

Bobby walked out on his porch leaning on the banister smoking a blunt. He saw a man in the alley peeing up against the building. Bobby got immediately agitated and started shouting. "Hey, Bruh, you better stop peeing on this building. Pee stinks in this heat!"

6

"I'm not your Bruh! I can pee wherever the hell I want!" the man alley yelled.

"You got one second to move," Bobby said with a menacing look on his face.

"Or what?" Bobby pulled out a gun, "Or you gonna feel this lead, bruh."

The man ran down the alley, holding onto his baggy pants. "Dude, over some piss? It ain't that serious!"

"You heard what the hell I said, and don't let me catch you again, or you will feel this lead!"

Debbie giggled as she leaned over the banister eating on a bag of flaming hots, sipping on a can of Busch beer.

"Looks like you scared him off."

"What's up, Debbie? I smell chicken. Where's my plate?" Bobby asked.

"All that weed you sell, you can buy a plate." "Oh, it's like that now?"

"Food ain't free, and they cut my benefits!" Debbie laughed. "You know I'm messing with you. How about this? I'll make you a nice plate if you hook me up with a nice ass bag of gas." "I got you, Debbie," Bobby said.

Janice walked through the gate, pushing Bobby Jr. in his stroller. She had bags hanging on the arms of the stroller and both her shoulders. She looked up. "Bobby, can you please come help me?"

Bobby was visibly annoyed by her request. He walked down the stairs slowly and lifted Bobby Jr from the stroller. "Where the hell you been?"

"I had to go to the WIC store (Women, Infants, and Children program)."

"Why you acting like you all handicap and shit." He pointed at the stroller. "Put the bags in the stroller, I got Bobby Jr. and carry it up. Damn, his diaper soaking wet!" Bobby carried Bobby Jr. up the stairs as Janice struggled to follow him with the stroller full of bags.

"He ran out of diapers. He has a few here, but I didn't have money on me to buy more."

7

"Your ass needs to get a job instead of sitting around here looking at these damn reality shows. Their reality is they already paid, and your broke ass ain't got shit." They reached their porch. Bobby pulled money from his pocket and threw it in Janice's face. "Go get my son some diapers."

Janice set down the stroller with the bags on their porch. She looked at the money with sadness on her face but made no move to pick it up. I don't have a sitter for Bobby Jr, how am I supposed to work? Daycare is not free. Are you going to watch him if I get a job? Hell, to the no, you not! Janice said frustrated.

"What the fuck you just say to me? Say that shit out loud, since you so bold." Bobby stared at Janice, with a menacing look on his face. "What was that?"

Janice raised her hands to cover her face. "I didn't say anything." "I didn't think you did. I ain't got time to be watching him. I'm out here hustling. Get Debbie, or old Ms. Noisy to watch him." Bobby stormed into their apartment with the baby, leaving Janice on their porch.

Vicky stepped out onto Ms. Ruby's porch as Ms. Ruby stepped out behind her settling in the chair. "Ms. Ruby, do you want me to cook you something before I leave?"

"No, child, I got some leftover meatloaf and some mashed potatoes I can warm up, but there is one thing I do need. The remote control fell back behind the couch. Can you get it for me? I want to look at that game show with that handsome man who host it."

"Yeah, Ms. Ruby, I'll get that remote for you. You know that brother talk show is taped here in Chicago, and he's making a lot of money. He got the game show, the talk show, and the show with the kids; and don't forget his books; I like the fact he gives a lot back to charities."

"Oh, I know, he's a rich man, just like my Scooter will be one day," Ms. Ruby said.

"I know that's right. Now when y'all come up, don't you forget about me, Ms. Ruby!" Vicky said. "I'm leaving now, but you just yell my name if you need me. Here's your remote." Vicky walked up the stairs to her back porch.

Bobby stepped out of his apartment and down the stairs to the alley, where he met JO-JO, a local thug who was wearing pants that were falling off his butt with timberland boots and a wife-beater t- shirt. They greeted each other with a handshake, then Bobby called up to Janice on the porch. "Hey, Janice!"

"What, Bobby?"

"Don't "what" me! Throw me that bag that's in the closet."

Janice walked inside the apartment and a moment later a duffel bag was tossed out the window to Bobby.

"So, Jo-Jo, you know I normally front you, but I can't front you on this shit. You got that money?"

"How long have you known me, Bob? You know I got the bread."

Jo-Jo pulled out a wad of money from his baggy pants pocket. "Alright, alright, I see you got my boys with you, Franklin and Grant." Bobby opened the duffel bag to show Jo-Jo the contents. "You like that, son?"

"That's what I'm talking about," Jo-Jo said.

"This Bobby's world, whatever you need, I got it" Jo-Jo gave Bobby a hand full of money and exited.

Scooter ran through the back gate, past Bobby, and up to his grandmother's porch. While Bobby entered his apartment.

"Grandma! Grandma!" Scooter yelled.

"Boy, what is it? What got you all fired up?"

"Scouts from UIC told Coach Johnson they been eyeing me. They said they like the way I play! Coach says they want me to come visit their school, to get a feel for the campus, the team, all that stuff," Scooter said excitedly. "Do you know what this means, Grandma?

That's a Division 1 school, and I could get a full ride!"

"A what, child?"

"A full ride, grandma! A scholarship! The scholarship will cover my books, room and board, supplies, and living expenses. I just have to keep my grades up and show up and show out on the field. Coach said other schools are interested too, but UIC is right here in town, Grandma! I'll be here, close to you."

Vicky stepped onto her porch as she heard the excitement in Scooter's voice.

Ms. Ruby gave Scooter a tight hug. "What I tell you, child? God will make away!"

"I know, Grandma! I need to go make some calls, let everyone know I'm going to college!"

Scooter gave Ms. Ruby another squeeze and then ran into their apartment.

Ms. Ruby held up her hands in praise. "Thank you, Jesus! Thank you, Jesus!"

"Sounds like you just got some good news, Ms. Ruby! Did I hear Scooter say he's playing college ball?" Vicky said.

"Yes ma'am, Vicky. My grandson going to college!"

A ring came from inside Ms. Ruby's apartment and Scooter stepped onto the porch holding their cordless phone. "Grandma, here, it's Coach Johnson."

Ms. Ruby took the phone from Scooter.

"Hello, Coach Johnson. I heard the good news from Scooter about a scholarship," Coach Johnson said. "Yes, Ma'am! The scouts have been keeping an eye on Scooter for quite some time now. With your permission, I'd like to take Scooter down for a visit, so he can get a feel of the school."

"That sounds okay with me, but how much will that cost, Coach Johnson?"

"Ms. Ruby, no need to worry about that. The expenses have been paid for; I just need your permission for him to go."

"Well if that's the case, and it's taken care of, Scooter has my permission," Ms. Ruby turned to look at Scooter, who was beaming.

"Great! We'll be leaving next Friday right after school, and we'll be returning that Sunday. Don't worry, he'll be safe with me."

"Oh, Coach, I'm not worried. I know you'll take good care of Scooter." Ms. Ruby hung up the phone. Scooter leaned in for another hug.

"Thank you, Grandma."

"Thank God, child, you finally got a chance to visit a school that wants to give you a scholarship! Didn't I say God was good? I said didn't I say God was good?"

"Grandma, I meant thank you for everything. Thank you for taking care of me and being by my side. This is my shot, Grandma, this is my shot," Scooter said.

"I hear you, Scooter. We got your back, the Lord and I." Ms. Ruby smiled as she touched Scooter's cheek affectionately.

"And I got faith you're going to get me that farm I dream about, too." Ms. Ruby chuckled.

Scooter headed back inside while Ms. Ruby sat on the porch. Janice came out to her porch across from Ms. Ruby, carrying Bobby Jr. "Hi, Ms. Ruby, Hey, Ms. Vicky."

"Bobby Jr. is getting big, pretty soon the boy will be in preschool."

"Yeah, he already eats like a grown man."

"It's good that he has a good appetite. What's not good is his daddy and the way he treats you. I hear y'all over there at night. A man like that, in Bobby's case, a boy who thinks he can scare a woman, not a man at all," Ms. Ruby said.

"She's telling the truth."

"It's not like that, though," Janice sighed.

"Oh, it's like that," Ms. Ruby said.

"We're not trying to gang up on you, Janice, we're on your side, but you need to start thinking about yourself too. If you keep letting him run over you and talk to you the way he does, he's going to think he's Ike Turner," Vicky said.

"Look, child, I know he's your baby daddy, but you need to start doing for you and Bobby Jr. Live the life you deserve to live."

Janice looked at her baby. "I don't know what to do, or how to do it. I don't know, I don't know." Janice shook her head. "Bobby and Bobby Jr. are all I know."

"Well, all I can say to that Janice is that you need to figure it out, Hell I had to," Vicky said.

"Ms. Vicky, that's easy for you to say. Mr. Willie is a good man, and he has a real job, and he loves you."

"She thinks I was born living with Willie," Vicky told Ms. Ruby, then she turned to Janice. "When I was around your age before I meet Willie, I was involved with a man who I thought loved me-- until he started beating on me and making me turn tricks." "Lord, Have Mercy! He what?!" Ms. Ruby asked.

"It started out with verbal abuse; then it went to him physically beating me, when I didn't make enough money. Because of him, I can't have children. I contracted PID (Pelvic inflammatory disease)."

"What's that?"

"Pelvic inflammatory disease is an infection of the female reproductive organs. Once contracted, your chances of having a baby are slim. "Vicky took a deep breath as she talked about her past.

"Vicky! You can't have children?!" Janice was surprised.

"Vicky, we talk about everything, you never told me this," Ms. Ruby said.

"I never told anyone, but Willie. We always said if we get a house one day, we will look into adopting a child."

"Mark my words, Vicky, the Lord is going to bless y'all with both a house and a child," Ms. Ruby said.

"So, Ms. Vicky, what happened? How did you get away from him? How did you meet Willie?"

"I set him up"

Janice looked puzzled, "You set him up?!" "So, what you do, child!?" Ms. Ruby asked.

"I called the police telling them he had drugs and counterfeit money stashed in the basement," Vicky said. "The next thing I know, they raided the place and took him to jail. Two years later, after getting my life back on track, I meet Willie. He was the first real man I can say I ever truly loved."

"So, with that being said, Bobby ain't no real man. He's a scared little boy in a man's body. I tell you what, you better start thinking about you and your son's future and forget about Bobby's wannabe gangster ass…Lord forgive my tongue!"

"I would like to go to school to become a nurse." "I always wanted to do that, then I found out I was pregnant. Lately, it seems like all I do is take care of Bobby and Bobby Jr." She hugged her baby, and kissed him softly on the cheeks. "At least one of them appreciates me."

"A nurse, now, I can see you doing that," Ms. Ruby said.

"After school, I would like to get a job working in the ER, open a bank account, save up money, and even get a house someday. (wistfully, longingly) A real house for me and my son. That's all I want, Ms. Ruby," Janice said.

"You'll make a great nurse, child! What's stopping you?" Ms. Ruby asked.

"I don't have help. I do not have a babysitter to watch Bobby Jr. long enough to shower, let alone spend all day at school. I can't afford daycare without a job."

"Bobby won't watch him - he too busy running the streets. I wouldn't have this apartment if it wasn't for Section 8. I get food stamps and a little check from the state, but it's just not enough for daycare," Janice started to tear up.

"Child, you got help right here, with Ms. Ruby." "And,

I can help too!" Vicky added.

"Ms. Ruby! Vicky!"

"I'll tell you what, I want you to go see about signing up for school, we got Bobby Jr. while you're gone." Ms. Ruby said.

Janice ran across the porch to hug Ms. Ruby and Vicky.

"It won't be easy, but you have God and two old women on your side."

"I'm not old yet!" Vicky said.

The women all laughed.

"Look, Janice, you're going through a storm right now, this is what we old folks call growing pains. Once that storm is over, you will feel the shine, but you must get through it first. You have to be strong to get through it." Ms. Ruby said.

"I want that for me and my baby boy. I want that clear sky, but Bobby not going to like me going to school."

"Besides yourself, there is one person to care about," Vicky said emphatically. "And, that's your son, Bobby Jr. Stop worrying about Bobby, he's a grown-ass man. As Ms. Ruby said, find your inner strength."

"I would like to go back to school and get my nursing degree to help take care of people like my grandma, who had Alzheimer's before she passed away." Janice sighed.

CHAPTER TWO

Later on that evening, Debbie sat on her porch preparing for one of her card parties. She was wiping the chairs and tables down when Vicky walked out onto her porch.

"Hey, Debbie, what you got going on?"

"It's gambling time. Do you want to get in?"

"I just might! Where's Roscoe?" Vicky took a seat at the table.

"He picked up some extra loads, you know how them truckers' schedules are, unpredictable."

"Yeah, I hear you. So, who all you invite over?"

"Gail?"

Vicky looked surprised. Debbie took a seat at the card table. "Gail! What about all that stuff that happened?"

"Frank was my boyfriend in high school, but that was a long time ago. She's still my cousin, and now he's her ex-husband." Debbie pulled out a deck of cards and started shuffling. "You remember, right after we graduated when I went down south to visit my grandparents?"

"Girl, that was so long ago."

"I was pregnant then," Debbie said. Vicky was incredulous, "Stop playing!"

"I'm not playing! I lost my baby when I was three months."

"So, your saying Frank got you pregnant?"

"Mm-hmm." Debbie shifted in her chair. "Frank did all his thinking with the head between his legs, but we all did dumb shit. Hell, we were young. Gail didn't steal him away, he went on his own. Girl, I should thank her! Frank was stepping out on Gail every chance he got. He ended up having kids outside their marriage, too."

Vicky was surprised, "Girl, no, he didn't!"

"Don't you go opening your mouth when Gail gets here. She went through enough with him already. He's in the hospital now. They say he

15

got that liver disease cirrhosis, so she brought her twins to see him. They say it's not looking good."

Bobby walked onto his porch, smoking a blunt. He leaned against the banister, talking on his cell phone. "What's up, bruh? Yeah, I got the shit. Alright! Cool, I'm out back. Hurry up, though, I'm leaving in a few." Bobby hung up his phone and blew smoke out his nostrils. Debbie leaned over her banister and called down to Bobby.

"Hey there, Bobby, I need some more weed, how much will a twenty get me?" Debbie asked.

Bobby laughed, "Two bags for the dub, Ms. Debbie. Let me grab it."

Bobby stepped into his apartment. Debbie turned to Vicky. "For the dub? What the hell is a dub?"

"A $20 bill Debbie, but you claim your hood," Vicky laughed.

Gail, Debbie's cousin came through the back gate wearing a yellow and white sundress with white flat sandals carrying a gift bag. She called out to Debbie as she started to climb the stairs. "Debbie, girl, I'm here!"

Debbie leaned over her banister and waved to Gail. "Hey, cuz!"

Gail reached Debbie's porch. "Girl, give me a hug! I haven't seen you since the family reunion!"

"How are the twins?"

"They're doing fine. I dropped them off at their daddy people's house."

"Hey, you remember Vicky, right?"

Gail set her gift bag down and took a seat at the card table. "Vicky, I haven't seen you in years, you still look nice."

"Hey, Gail! You're looking nice too, girl."

Debbie playfully poked at the gift bag. "Cuz, what's in the bag?"

"I know you like your drinks, so I brought you some hundred-proof moonshine."

"Oh, we city folks up here, what the hell is Moonshine?" They all laughed.

"A drink that will have you on your ass. Now shuffle them dang on cards so I can take you chicks money," Gail said.

Bobby exited his apartment and walked up the steps to Debbie's porch. "Here you go, Ms. Debbie." Bobby handed Debbie two plastic bags of weed, and she handed him the twenty.

"And here's your dub, Bobby,". Vicky shook her head.

Bobby walked back downstairs to his apartment.

"That's what I'm talking about! Time to put it in the air." Debbie begins to roll up a fat joint.

"Since when did you start smoking?" Gail asked.

"I smoke every now and then. You!"

"I just recently started smoking ever since I been going through this shit with Frank."

"Wow, cuz, I would never have thought you smoked."

Hours had passed, and the women were finishing up their card game.

"It's one in the morning, can you say tipsy! I'm about to go home and lay it down," Vicky said.

"Nice seeing you again Vicky."

"You mean, nice taking my money."

"Yeah, that too," Gail chuckled. "Goodnight,

Vicky," Debbie said.

Vicky stood up and returned to her apartment. Gail and Debbie sat in awkward silence.

"Listen, Debbie, I have to tell you something I should have said a long time ago."

"Now, Gail, I know where this is going."

"Just let me talk, okay? We were all children, and I was dumb. I didn't know you and Frank were serious. I thought you were just one of those girls chasing the star basketball player. That's what he told me."

"Gail, look, there is no need for all this. Like you said, we were children. We're grown now! The cheating, the pregnancy, that was all a long time ago."

"The pregnancy!"

"Damn, I didn't mean to let that slip out. Blame it on the alcohol." Damn moonshine!

Gail looked surprised. "Pregnancy, what pregnancy? Frank got you pregnant?!"

"Yes, but I lost the baby. I was three months."

"Debbie, I wish I had known. That man was always a hoe. Hell, that's why I divorced his trifling ass." Gail grabbed a joint from the ashtray and lit it up. "Did you ever tell him?"

"Nope!"

Gail nodded her head slowly and took a hit. "Frank was a headache you avoided. I love our twins, but Frank and all his cheating, I couldn't take it anymore. I didn't deserve to be treated the way he treated me." Gail passed Debbie the joint.

"I'm sorry you had to go through that, especially him having other children behind your back." Debbie took a hit off the joint, while both women sat in silence.

Gail looked at her watch. "Cuz, it's late, I'm going to head out." Gail gathered her things.

CHAPTER THREE

It was morning as Debbie walked out of her apartment and called down to Ms. Ruby, who sat on her porch sipping on her coffee. "Hey there, Ms. Ruby! Did you get a letter from the city, about the building?"

"I got mail but haven't opened it yet. What's going on?" Ms. Ruby asked.

"The city says the building has a lot of code violations. If Davis Jr. doesn't get things fixed around here, the building can be shut down and we may have to move," Debbie replied

"Oh, I can't say I'm surprised. When Davis Sr. owned the place, the building was in good standards, but when Davis Jr. took over, the building's been going down ever since."

"He's a straight slumlord."

Vicky exited her apartment and walked down the stairs to Ms. Ruby's porch.

"Vicky, did you hear about the building violations?" Ms. Ruby asked her.

"Willie was just telling me about it. We've been wanting to move anyways." Vicky took a seat. "The roof leaks when it rains. We got bugs. The building's front door has been broken for a while. Paint peeling off the walls. I'm tired of the roaches. I even seen mice droppings."

Debbie walked to the top step taking a seat looking down at Ms. Ruby and Vicky as she puffed on a cigarette as she sipped on a beer. "I hear you, Vicky. This building has gone downhill since the gambler Davis Jr. took over."

"I would love to move to find someplace nice for Scooter and me, but with my Social Security check, it's hard to save." Ms. Ruby sighed. "But God got a plan for all of us, mark my words."

Janice stepped onto her porch, stretching her arms to the sky. "Morning, ladies."

"Good morning, child. Where's that baby of yours?" Ms. Ruby asked.

"He's still sleeping. Hey, I went to the library to use the computer and I seen some good nursing programs. I decided that I'm going to go up to the school and talk with a counselor about enrolling." "Now, child, that's what I'm talking about! I'm proud of you. Now, if you put in the work, God will get you through. I'll watch Bobby Jr, just bring him enough diapers."

"He can be a little messy at times. I'll bring some extra clothes to Ms. Ruby. Should I bring some food over too? "

"Nah, I think I can put something together he can eat. Remember, I got a grandson, too. Just make sure he got his bottle, I can handle the rest," Ms. Ruby said.

"I'm going to tell Bobby that I'm going to look for a job, and you're going to watch Bobby Jr. while I look, okay Ms. Ruby."

"Child, tell him whatever you need, just make sure you go take care of business with that school." Vicky and Ms. Ruby both nodded in agreement.

Bobby yelled from inside the apartment. A few minutes later, he stepped onto the porch. "Janice, where you at?"

"Boy, can't you talk in a normal tone?" Ms. Ruby frowned. Vicky and Debbie disappeared into their apartments. Ms. Ruby sipped her coffee as Bobby looked towards her.

"Hi, Ms. Ruby." Bobby looked at Janice. "Janice, did you get the link? We don't have any bacon or eggs?"

"Yeah, I got it."

"So, where's the damn food? You got the link, so why haven't you been to the store? Got me in here starving."

"I still haven't gotten Bobby Jr. together, plus I got the laundry to do. Can you run to the store, please?"

"Yeah, Bobby, how about you run to the store, and while you're there, you can play my lottery too?" Ms. Ruby added.

"I'll go since you asked, Ms. Ruby. Let me brush my teeth and throw on a shirt, I'll be ready in a few minutes." Bobby walked back into the apartment.

Janice said in a relieved tone. "Thank you, Ms. Ruby."

"Child, learn to stand up for yourself."

"I will, Ms. Ruby, I will!"

Faint crying came from inside the apartment.

"I think I hear that baby of yours."

"Yeah, let me go check on him. Thanks again, Ms. Ruby. I'll talk to you later."

Bobby exited the apartment as Janice went in.

"Ms. Ruby, you got your lottery numbers ready?" Bobby asked.

"Hold on, I'll have Scooter grab them off my dresser." She shouted, "Scooter!" Scooter stuck his head out of the door.

"Yes, Grandma?"

"Grab them lottery tickets off my dresser with that $20 bill."

Scooter disappeared into the apartment and walked back out to the porch with the lottery tickets and the $20 bill in hand. "Here you go, Grandma. Hey, what up, Bobby?"

"What up, Mr. Football star? I heard your team won." "Yeah, we stamped the yard on them, boys."

"That's what's up? I remember when I played football." "You played football, Bobby? What Happened?"

"Let's just say, you have a coach and a Grandma who got your back. I had a daddy who was an alcoholic who beat my back. Anyways, I heard your team is hitting the Pizza Bowl."

"Yeah, the coach brother owns the place, so he's letting us eat free pizza and bowl to celebrate. Can you say smash time?" Scooter rubbed his stomach, then headed back into the apartment.

Bobby took Ms. Ruby's tickets and headed to the store. Debbie exited her apartment and leaned over her balcony, cigarette in hand. "Oooooh Weeeee, it is nice out here."

Ms. Ruby sat in her chair doing her crossword puzzle. "Yes, I must say it is. Did you thank God for waking you up and allowing you to see another day?"

"Ms. Ruby, I do that every day. I thank my heavenly father, and then I—"

"Then you what? Open a beer?"

"No, Ma'am! I brush my teeth, wash my face, and then I grab a beer." Debbie laughed.

"Well, you best be careful drinking like you do on these raggedly porches."

"Do you think I could sue Davis Jr. if I fall?" "Child, we both know he ain't got no money."

"You right, you right."

Bobby returned. "Ms. Ruby here's your lottery tickets."

Ms. Ruby took her tickets as she frowned, "Boy, my tickets smell like that stuff."

"What stuff?" Bobby asked.

"Don't play like you slow now! You know what stuff I'm talking about. That garbage you be selling and smoking."

"Ms. Ruby, you smell my cigarettes. I had them in my pocket with your tickets."

"Listen here, boy, I may be old, but I still got my sense of smell. I know the difference between cigarettes and that stuff. I'll tell you something else, you keep messing with that stuff, your gonna end up in jail."

"Ms. Ruby, they got to catch me first."

"Mm-hmm! A hard head makes a soft behind! Thanks for playing my lottery through."

Bobby entered his apartment as Scooter stepped out onto the porch. "Okay, Grandma, I'm about to head out to the Pizza Bowl with the guys."

"Okay, you got your phone and your keys? I'll be asleep by the time you get home."

"Yes, Grandma, I got my keys and phone." Scooter walked down the stairs and exited.

Debbie leaned over the banister. "Mrs. Ruby, that grandson of yours is going to be finer than wine when he gets older. He's lucky, I'm too old for him, or I would show him a few things."

"Child, what you got to show him? Nothing!"

Debbie started to sing, "I don't see nothing wrong with a little bump and grind." Debbie grabbed the banister and swayed her hips.

"Debbie, don't let me have to cane you down about my Grandson." Ms. Ruby pointed her cane in the air towards Debbie.

"Ah, Ms. Ruby, you know I'm just playing with you."

"Mm-hmm."

"Anyways, my friend and I are heading down to play some bingo at the bar in a bit, would you like to go?" Debbie asked.

"A bar? Nah, Debbie, I don't hang out in the devil's house. I'm about to watch this gospel program and snack on some hot meat and crackers."

"Okay, Ms. Ruby, you enjoy your hot meat and gospel."

"I will! You enjoy your evening and be careful out there. Every day it's something happening in this city."

Ms. Ruby and Debbie both entered their apartments, as Bobby stepped onto his porch lighting up a blunt. "I see it's getting dark, time to go make this money."

Janice exited the apartment carrying Bobby Jr. on her hip. "Bobby, I'm about to leave out. Frankie's throwing her son a birthday party and I'm taking Bobby Jr."

"I hope you got your keys; I won't be here when you get back." "I got 'em."

CHAPTER FOUR

It was Sunday morning and some of the tenants were preparing to go to church.

Willie stepped out onto his porch sipping on a cup of Joe. "It sure feels good out here this morning."

Bobby stepped onto his porch and threw a bag of garbage over the banister. "What's good, Willie?"

"This weather. How's Bobby Jr.?"

"He's good! Janice took him to a birthday party last night. I guess they spent the night over at Janice's friend house."

"That's shocking, Janice is always home."

"Yeah, I came in this morning, and they were still gone. My phone died and my charger broke so, I don't know if she called or not. I'm sure she just stayed over her best friend Frankie's house after the party."

Ms. Ruby stepped onto her porch, humming a song.

"Good morning, Ms. Ruby."

"Good morning, Bobby! You up early."

"Always up early, like a rooster."

"Janice and your baby still sleeping?"

"Nah, they're not here. I think she stayed over her friend Frankie's house last night after the kid's birthday party."

"Oh, okay! Look, I need to have a word with you, child."

"Maybe later Ms. Ruby, I have to go buy a charger for my phone. Missed calls mean missed money. I'm heading up to the gas station. I'll holler at you when I get back."

'Please don't forget! I really have something I need to talk to you about,".

"Okay, Ms. Ruby." Bobby stepped off the porch and exited.

Debbie stepped onto her porch with rollers in her hair, eating a bowl of cereal. "Hey, Ms. Ruby."

"Good morning, child. Are you going to church today?"

Debbie patted her hair rollers. "Yes, Ma'am, got my rollers in my hair, and clothes laid out on the bed. You know them church folks be looking people up and down, judging everybody that walks through them doors."

"Child, the Lord says, "come as you are." No need to be trying to impress folks. The only one you should be worried about is the Lord above. People going to talk regardless, hell they talked about Jesus Christ."

"I know Ms. Ruby, but If they want something to judge, I'm gonna give them something to talk about. I'll be ready in just a few." Debbie drank down the milk from her cereal bowl and headed inside to finish getting ready.

Vicky stepped onto her porch walking down to Ms. Ruby. "Morning Ms. Ruby! Are you ready for church today?"

"Yes, Vicky, I'm always ready to go to the Lord's house. I smelled your cakes in my sleep. I almost bit my lip off." Ms. Ruby chuckled.

"Yeah, I was up baking all night. I baked three cakes and three dozen cupcakes for the church bake sale."

"Your cakes and cupcakes are definitely going to sell out. Let me wake this boy up so he can start getting ready." Ms. Ruby called into her apartment. "Scooter, baby. It's time to get up!"

Silence…

"He must be knocked out," Vicky said.

Ms. Ruby called again. "Scooter, I said it's time for church!" "I know this boy hears me." Ms. Ruby looked at Vicky.

Ms. Ruby stepped into the apartment and then returned. "Ms. Ruby, you get him up?"

"I guess he didn't come home last night. He didn't even call me to tell me he was staying out. Let me get my phone and call him."

"Ms. Ruby, he's a good kid, I'm sure he just spent the night over at one of the player's houses. What's his best friend name? Mickey. They

25

probably stayed up late playing those video games," Vicky said reassuringly.

Ms. Ruby dialed Scooter's number. After a few moments, unable to reach Scooter, she lowered the phone. "I know his team was celebrating, but he could've called me to let me know he was staying out," Ms. Ruby said worryingly.

"I'm quite sure he's okay, Ms. Ruby. He may still be sleeping. By the time we get back from church, he should be here."

"I guess you may be right. Let me slip on my shoes and grab my Bible." Ms. Ruby walked back into her apartment. Vicky walked up the stairs to her apartment.

Vicky called Willie. "Willie, come grab the cakes and cupcakes and take them down to the car. I'll lock the door and will get Debbie."

Willie came out of the apartment carrying boxes down the stairs. Vicky locked the door then walked over to knock on Debbie's door.

"I hear you, girl. I'm coming!" Debbie said. She stepped out onto the porch as if she was stepping out onto a runway wearing knee- high red boots that were hugging her thick thighs, with a black mini skirt and a black see-through lace shirt sporting a red bra under it.

"Debbie, we're going to church, not the club!" Vicky said.

"Girl, don't hate because I'm looking flawless. I'm going to give them church folks something to talk about and remember."

Ms. Ruby exited her apartment with her Bible in hand and locks the door.

Vicky, Debbie, and Ms. Ruby all exited out the back gate.

CHAPTER FIVE

It was later the same day. Ms. Ruby and Vicky had just returned from the hospital.

"Thank God he's going to be okay," Vicky said in a relieved tone.

"Yes, Lord, thank you, Jesus, He's alive, but why wouldn't they let me stay?" Ms. Ruby, said in a frustrated, nervous tone, emphatically. "My grandson needs me!" Ms. Ruby took a seat in the chair on her porch.

Vicky told her in a soothing voice, "Ms. Ruby, he's in intensive care. They'll be moving him to a regular room soon enough, and you can stay with him then; you need your rest, your legs are in no shape to be sitting up in those tight butt hospital chairs with your legs in pain. You may be right, but I'm going to need...

Vicky interrupted, "I'll take you back up to the hospital first thing in the morning Ms. Ruby. You just get some rest first. Scooter is going to need you to be strong for him."

"Child, I do appreciate you." Ms. Ruby smiled!

Debbie stepped onto her porch with a beer in hand. She called down to Ms. Ruby and Vicky. "Is everything okay?"

"Scooter was shot in the upper shoulder, there was another boy who was killed. You know, Janice was there too, but we don't know why. It was so much going on," Vicky said.

"Shut your mouth! Bobby baby mommy Janice? What the hell!? Ms. Ruby, is Scooter okay? Are you, okay?" Debbie said.

"My grandson is alive. The doctors say he might have some nerve damage, and he'll probably have to do rehab to get his nerves back right in his arm."

"Scooter's a strong boy. He'll be okay," Debbie said. "Debbie, has Bobby been back?" Vicky asked.

"I haven't seen him since he ran out of the gate earlier," Debbie said.

"This city just isn't safe. All the drugs, the gangs, the guns. When is it all going to end? Satan got his hooks in this city, but my God, he's watching over us. Lord, please spread your blessing and your guidance over this whole city. We need your help, Lord. We need your covering," Ms. Ruby said as she stretched her hands to the sky.

Bobby came running through the gate and up the stairs. Once he reached his porch he paced back and forth. "I'm going to find out who did this, and when I do, they're going to feel this lead." Bobby displayed the gun on the side of his waist.

"That attitude is not going to solve a thing," Ms. Ruby said. "Now, Vicky and I saw Janice at the hospital, but it was so much going on, we never got a chance to ask her what happened. So, what happened, why was Janice there?"

"I just know Janice took Bobby Jr. to the pizza bowl for a party, and it was a shooting, and Bobby Jr. got grazed by one of the bullets. I'm gonna kill whoever did this." Bobby pulled the gun from his waist.

"And then what do you plan on doing once you find out? Kill them? What is that going to solve? You shoot them, then they come back, they shoot and kill you, then your boys go out to shoot them, and the cycle continues," Ms. Ruby said. "Look, my grandson was shot in that shooting too, and it's sad to say, these children are the ones doing the shooting and killing, but retaliation is not the answer. Now, put that gun away, and just pray that your son will be fine," she added empathically, pleading.

Bobby's voice was full of anger, "Pray, old lady? pray? What the hell am I praying for? That so-called God of yours ain't never did anything for me! I've been beaten, abused, and bounced from foster home to foster home. Your so-called God never gave me anything. The streets and making money are all I know!" Bobby pulled a stack of money from his pocket. "I will find out who did this," Bobby said in a firm, aggressive tone. He ran off the porch and exited.

CHAPTER SIX

Several months had passed. Debbie walked out of her apartment, and leaned on her porch rail stuffing pancakes into her mouth, looking down at Ms. Ruby, who sat relaxing in her chair enjoying a cup of coffee.

"Good morning, Ms. Ruby!"

"Morning, Debbie."

"So, what do you have planned this morning?"

"I'm just enjoying my coffee while Scooter gets ready for therapy."

"So, how is his therapy coming?" Debbie sat on the top step looking down at Ms. Ruby as she placed the empty plate next to her, and lit up a cigarette

"He's progressing one day at a time. He still has some damaged nerves, but with time, it should get better."

Scooter stepped out onto the porch and kissed Ms. Ruby on the cheek. "Good morning, Grandma." He took a seat on the porch. "Morning, Ms. Debbie."

"Hey, Scooter, how you doing?"

"I'm doing okay, Ms. Debbie." Scooter rotated his shoulder gingerly, then winced. "I'll be back on the field any day now."

"God is going to heal you Scooter, you just need a mustard seed of faith…"

"Yeah, yeah, I know he can move mountains, Grandma," Scooter said in a sarcastic voice.

Debbie looked at Ms. Ruby, in shock.

"Look, boy, I know you're upset about your arm, but you better watch your mouth," Ms. Ruby said sternly.

"Sorry, grandma!"

"Mmm hmm! Now, would you like me to fix you some breakfast?"

"No, grandma, I'm going to eat some cereal. Coach is on his way to pick me up. He says they found some specialist for me to see about my arm."

"A specialist?" Ms. Ruby asked.

"All I know, Grandma, is that the coach said he works with people like me who have nerve damage. He's even worked with some top college players, and some NFL players, too."

"See, the Lord is already working miracles for you!"

"Yeah, we'll see. I need to go eat and take my meds before Coach gets here." Scooter stepped back into the apartment.

"I never heard him talk like that, but I understand he's upset. He'll pull through this Ms. Ruby," Debbie said.

Janice walked out onto her porch. "Good morning, Debbie. Ms. Ruby.

"Morning, child, how's that sweet baby of yours?" back."

"He's still sleeping, but he's finally starting to get his appetite

"That's good! Glad to hear he's doing better," Debbie looked at her watch. She then glanced at her phone. "Lord, look at the time. You, ladies, have a good day." Debbie grabbed her plate and walked into her apartment.

"Ms. Ruby, I would like to say thank you again, for being so helpful with Bobby Jr these past few months. Your prayers and your support are helping us get through," Janice said.

"Child, don't thank me, the Lord did all the work. All I did was ask him to watch over you."

Vicky walked out onto her porch. "Morning, Ms. Ruby. Let me just make Willie some breakfast and then I'll be down to take Scooter to rehab."

"No need today, Vicky. His coach is picking him up to go see some specialist that works with damaged nerves."

"Well, that's good! A specialist is what Scooter may need besides what the county is providing. So, did you ever hear anything back from the police?"

"Not a thing. I called the detective a few days ago and he said they're still looking for the shooter, but he said they are following up on a few good leads," Ms. Ruby said.

"Well, I sure hope they find him, and put him under the jail," Vicky said.

"Janice, have you heard back from the police?" Ms. Ruby said. "My phone been off, and Bobby doesn't keep the same number so, I wouldn't know. I tried calling them a while back but was told they're following up on some leads."

Muffled cries come from inside Janice's apartment. "Bobby Jr's awake, time to feed him." Janice walked back into her apartment.

Ms. Ruby's, phone rang, it was a call from Coach Johnson. "Morning, Ms. Ruby! So, did Scooter tell you the news about the specialist?"

"Good morning, Coach! He told me something about a specialist helping him with his arm but can you tell me more?"

"Yes, Ma'am, the coaching staff at UIC recommended this guy. They can't help with any rehab until he's officially on campus, but they suggested we use him."

"So, the school still wants Scooter to play, coach?"

"That all depends on how Scooter's therapy goes, but they haven't given up on him. They still want him to play, but he has to get back healthy first."

"Coach, my insurance is barely paying for his rehab, I don't know if I can pay for a specialist."

"We're in luck there. Turns out this therapist isn't just great at his job, he's also a fan of Scooters. That grandson of yours is a local hero.

You have a talented grandson there, Ma'am. He already has the most yards in high school quarterback history; he has the most touchdowns thrown by a high school quarterback, and let's not forget, he was the MVP for two straight years. So, Ms. Ruby, you don't have to worry about anything--we got him covered. We want to see Calvin recover 100%. We got him; don't you worry."

"Okay, I hear you coach! So, what can this specialist do that's different from what the rehab center has been doing?" Ms. Ruby said.

31

"He'll be handling all of Scooter's physical therapy, and he also agreed to organize Scooter's psychiatric counseling. A lot of athletes can't cope with an injury like this, and just give up. I know Scooter's a strong young man, and he's got you to lean on, but this specialist can help even more including with pain management."

"Well, coach, since we don't have to pay, and this will help Scooter get better, I suppose he can start seeing the specialist." Scooter stepped out onto the porch. "Bye, Grandma."

"Ms. Ruby, if you want to meet the specialist, you're more than welcome to come," Coach Johnson said.

"No Coach, I trust you. Plus, I'm going to sit here and rub this stinky cream on my knees."

CHAPTER SEVEN

It was morning, three months later. Ms. Ruby sat on her porch highlighting passages in her Bible as Scooter walked onto the porch, eating a bowl of cereal. "Good morning, Grandma."

"Morning Scooter! You look tired. You didn't get enough sleep?" "I'm okay, this therapy," he sighed. "It's just harder than I thought it would be."

"It may seem hard now, but trust me, it will pay off at the end, and you'll be back on that field before you know it," Ms. Ruby said. "I remember your mommy saying she knew you were going to be a football player." Ms. Ruby smiled at the memory and continued marking in her Bible.

"I miss my mama, too," Scooter said sadly.

"I know you do. I do too! But trust me, her spirit is here with us." "You think she still sees a ballplayer in me?"

"Trust me, Scooter, she's proud of you, and so am I. You're going to get through this therapy and come back stronger than ever, mark my words."

"I hope so, grandma. My future depends on it." "My shoulder hurts. I'm going to take a pill and lift weights." Scooter went back into the apartment, as Janice stepped onto her porch with her backpack in her hand.

"Good morning, Ms. Ruby."

"Morning, child! What you got there homework?"

Janice took a seat on her porch pulling out a textbook from her backpack.

"No, just some studying. Bobby, Jr. is still sleeping, and I figured that I'd get some studying done before he woke up. I'm glad I took your advice, Ms. Ruby. Going back to school is one of the best decisions I ever made."

Willie exited his apartment and walked down the stairs. He stopped at Ms. Ruby's porch. "Good morning, Ms. Ruby! Good morning, Janice."

"Hey, Mr. Wille!" Janice said.

"You heading off to work, Wille?" Ms. Ruby asked.

"Yes, Ms. Ruby, off to work I go. Do you need me to bring you anything when I get off?"

"Yes! Some Epsom Salt. These knees of mine are aching and swollen." Ms. Ruby rubbed her knees.

"Will do, Ms. Ruby." Willie walked down the stairs and exited.

Bobby stepped out onto the back porch.

"Janice, Bobby Jr. is awake. You need to get in here and feed him."

"Can't you see I'm studying, Bobby? He's your son, too. Can you feed him, please?" Janice said annoyed.

"Yeah, Bobby, she's studying. Can you feed him?"

"I'll feed him, but you need to hurry up, I got moves and money to make." Bobby stepped back into the apartment.

Vicky stepped onto her porch looking down at Ms. Ruby with a can of soda in her hand. "Ms. Ruby, will you still be needing a ride to your doctor's appointment?"

"Yes, child, I'm still going. These old legs of mine need some looking at. They are swelling worse than ever." Ms. Ruby struggled to lift herself out of her chair using the banister.

Janice ran down the stairs to Ms. Ruby. "Aww, Ms. Ruby. Let me help you!"

"Child, a little pain won't stop me. I may be old, but I ain't handicapped." Ms. Ruby looks up at Vicky. "Let me go in here and get dressed, Vicky. I'll be ready in a few." Ms. Ruby entered her apartment.

CHAPTER EIGHT

It was hours later as Ms. Ruby and Vicky returned from the doctor's appointment. Ms. Ruby was now using a four-prong cane to walk, along with Vicky's assistance.

Debbie saw this from her porch and came down the stairs to help. "Ms. Ruby, are you okay?" Debbie reached Ms. Ruby and took her by the arm to assist her.

"I'm okay, child! These legs just don't work like they used to." "She's gonna be fine," Vicky said.

The women reached Ms. Ruby's porch, helping her into her chair.

Vicky pulled out the keys and unlocked Ms. Ruby's door.

"What did the doctor say about your legs, Ms. Ruby?" Debbie asked. "The doctor says I got the veins."

"The veins? What the heck is the veins?"

"Doctor says I got varicose veins and bad arthritis." "Aww, Ms. Ruby, I'm sorry to hear that," Debbie said.

"Child, I'm going to be just fine. I got God by my side, and I got medication to help with the pain. I have an appointment to go see a vascular specialist, so I'll be just fine." Ms. Ruby started to hum.

"Okay, Ms. Ruby, I'm gonna head on upstairs, you just call me if you need me," Vicky said.

"Thank you, Vicky, take this." Ms. Ruby pulled money out of her bra handing, it to Vicky.

"Now, Ms. Ruby, you put that money away!" Vicky walked up the stairs and into her apartment.

"Ms. Ruby, you can call me too, if you need anything. Unlike Vicky, I won't turn down your money." Debbie walked up to her porch, laughing. "I'm just joking, Ms. Ruby! I'm here if you need me to."

Debbie entered her apartment.

CHAPTER NINE

The following day, Janice stepped out onto her porch and began hanging laundry. Scooter walked through the gate and stumbled up onto the porch. "Scooter, you okay?" "I'm fine!"

"Where have you been?" Ms. Ruby asked.

"Grandma, please stop treating me like a child. I'm 18 years old and I'm not a little boy," Scooter said frustratedly. "But, since you asked, I was out with my boys." His voice returned to its normal tone. "Anyways, the coach is on his way, he's taking some of us to the orientation."

Ms. Ruby sat looking puzzled, "I was just asking."

"Orientation okay, you're almost there, on your way to becoming a college student. Now, don't let these girls distract you, and take your dreams away like Bobby distracted me," Janice said.

Scooter looked at them but ignored Janice's comment. "That's my Scooter. My grandson ain't going to let nothing and no one distract him."

"I have to take a shower and get dressed." Scooter stepped into the apartment.

"What's wrong with him?" Janice said.

"Ever since the shooting, his attitude has changed. He seems so distant." Ms. Ruby sighed, in a resigned tone. "All I can do is pray for him and ask God to guide him."

"Hmm, I just never seen him like that or heard him talk like that before," Janice said.

Coach Johnson called Ms. Ruby on the phone. Ms. Ruby picked up her cordless phone as it began to ring. "Hi there, Ms. Ruby!"

"How you doing there, Coach? Scooter tells me you're taking him to the school for freshmen orientation. I surely appreciate you!"

"Yes, Ma'am! I'll be taking him and a few more players who were accepted," Coach Johnson said. "I have a question for you, has Scooter seemed a bit different to you lately?"

"We were just talking about that. The boy seems to be distant lately, and somewhat irritated."

"I told you Scooter seemed different," Janice said in the background.

"I'm not sure what's going on yet. He's not as pumped as he was before. I'll talk to him after I drop the other boys off. Can you tell him to come down, and I'll talk with you later Ms. Ruby?"

"Scooter, your coach is here!" Ms. Ruby yelled.

"I'll see you later, Grandma." Scooter headed down the stairs and out the gate.

Bobby walked onto the porch, with his cell phone to his ear as Janice took the laundry back into their apartment. "Dude, you better have my damn money when I get over there, or we're going to have problems!" Bobby hung up his phone.

"Boy, you watch your mouth, I know you see me sitting here," Ms. Ruby said. "So, you making a drug deal?"

"There you go, all up in my business again."

"Look, boy, I tell you that fast life is not the life to live. People who live that fast money life end up in one of two places: dead or in jail."

"Now, Ms. Ruby, I got this here, and besides, what am I supposed to do? Go get a job that pays minimum wage, where I have to work like a slave to receive a check that barely pays a bill--not the bills but a bill? I got a son! I take care of my crib, thanks to these streets." Bobby walked down the stairs and exited through the gate.

Debbie walked out of her apartment down to Ms. Ruby's. "Ms. Ruby, as my mommy use to say to me, 'You can lead the boy to the toilet, but he has to learn how to aim.'"

"I ain't never heard it put like that, but I guess it makes sense."

Janice walked out onto the porch placing Bobby Jr. in his playpen and reading mail. "Hello, ladies!"

"Hi, Janice! Have you received mail from the city about the building?" Debbie asked.

"About the building? Yeah, I got it. Something about code violations. Bobby said we're going to move as soon as he gets his money right," Janice said.

"Child, concentrate on your baby and school. After you finish school, trust me, you will get a job. Once you get a job, you can get your own place, without Bobby."

"Janice, she's right! Finish school and the rest will follow," Debbie said.

Debbie headed upstairs to her apartment. Janice went through her mail. She pulled out a letter and looked it over with excitement on her face.

Janice opened the envelope and starts reading. "Oh, my goodness! I don't believe this," she said excitedly

"What you got there child?" Ms. Ruby asked. "It's a letter from my mother."

"Your mother who you said was in jail?"

"Yes, Ms. Ruby, I only got one!" Janice chuckled.

"So, what the letter saying, child? How'd she find you?" Ms. Ruby asked.

"That's a good question. I don't know how she found out where I live." She started reading the letter. "It says she wants to see me."

CHAPTER TEN

Vicky sat out on her porch as Ms. Ruby stepped onto her porch using her cane. Vicky called down to Ms. Ruby when she heard Ms. Ruby's screen door open and close.

"Hey, Ms. Ruby! Did you hear the news?"

"What news is that, child?"

Vicky walked down to Ms. Ruby's porch as Ms. Ruby took a seat. "About the building. Mr. Davis doesn't own it anymore. The new owner is stopping by today, to talk to us all regarding the new management of the building."

"I ain't heard a thing about that. How did you hear about it?" Ms. Ruby asked.

"Well, I was in front of the building earlier, and there were two men looking around, sticking up signs. So, you know me, I had to ask what was going on, and the young man said, 'Hi, Ma'am,' and I was like, 'Hi, is there something I can help you with because it looked like he was pushing up on the door. I told him the door doesn't work, and it hasn't in a long time. He said he and some workers will be over here, later on, to start doing some work on the building, and he would like to have a tenant meeting with us, while he's around. I told him the best time would be this afternoon," Vicky said.

"Did you get the new owner's name?" Ms. Ruby asked.

"He's one of those guys with two first names, Mr. Levi James.

Funny timing, Willie and I were just talking about finding a new place to move."

"I hear you, child. As bad as I'd like to move, it would be hard for me now, considering I don't have anything saved up, and my Social Security check can only stretch so far. I hope, whoever he is, that he'll get this building back right, you know, how it use to be."

"He seemed like a nice guy, Ms. Ruby."

"I hope so. This whole building needs a makeover."

"He said they will be back after picking up supplies for the building."

"Finally, no more Davis Jr," Ms. Ruby said happily. She rubbed her legs, as Bobby walked out onto their porch as Janice walked behind him holding Bobby Jr. in her arms.

"But, Bobby, I want to go,".

"What the hell you want to go see her for? She ain't been here for you all these years."

"Bobby, she's my mom. I got a lot of questions to ask her. Things like, do she know where my daddy is? If she knows if I really got other siblings? How long she's been clean?"

"And if she's still sucking that glass dick."

Janice rolled her eyes. "Can't you just be happy for me? Look I know your mom passed but what if your dad called you out of the blue, wouldn't you want to talk to him, and ask questions?"

"Man, fuck that dude. He ain't done shit for me. The only motherfucker I want to see is these Benjamins." Bobby pulled a wad of money out of his pockets." Bobby said angrily. "Me and Bobby Jr. are your family. You better not take my son around that dope fiend or I'm going to whoop your ass like Satin whooped Sparkle." "But, Bobby!" Janice pleaded.

"But Bobby, nothing! I don't want to talk about it no more. You heard what the hell I said!" Bobby said angrily. He raised his hand towards Janice with a frown and headed out the gate.

Ms. Ruby addressed Janice. "Child, is everything okay?"

"Bobby, he gets on my nerves!" Janice said frustratedly. "I'm so tired of him, he acts like he's my daddy! If I want to see my mom and want her to meet my son, her grandchild, that's on me!"

"Janice, you take that boy to see his grandma. Don't let that Bobby discourage you from doing what's in your heart." "That's right!" Vicky said.

"Remember that letter I got from her? She said she's been looking for me for a while now!" Janice said.

"Time for you to get your answers. Time for you to get to know your mother and the things and struggles she's been through. Your answers lay with your mother, child." Ms. Ruby said.

"She says she's been clean for some time now. She's also a drug counselor and teaches Sunday school."

"See how God can change lives?!" Ms. Ruby said.

"Where do she stay Janice?" Vicky asked

"She's married, they stay out in the suburbs. She wants me to come out to her church. You know, that huge one off the expressway on the west side. She also said she got a surprise for me."

"Again, Janice, it's time. Go see your mother and take your son with you." She grabbed Janice's hand, it's time.

"Speaking of change, here comes Mr. James," Vicky said. "Who is Mr. James?" Janice asked.

"The building's new owner," Vicky said.

Mr. James entered the back of the building walking up the stairs to Ms. Ruby's porch looking like bubba off of Sandford and Son wearing a white dress shirt, some flooded dress pants, white socks with penny loafer shoes. "Ahh, hello, ladies., my name is Levi James.

I'm the new landlord of this building." Mr. James pointed at Vicky. "Hello, again, Ma'am!"

"You can call me Vicky! I was just telling the ladies about you."

Debbie stepped onto her porch walking down the stairs towards the other ladies, filing her nails popping bubble gum. "Yes, Mr. James, Vicky was telling us about you. So, what happened to Mr. Davis?"

"Debt happened. He let the building go into foreclosure. I bought the building from the bank. And your name, Ma'am?"

"I'm Debbie, I stay upstairs over Ms. Ruby." Debbie slowly looked Mr. James up and down.

"I'm Janice, and this is my baby, Bobby Jr. We stay here right across from Ms. Ruby."

Everyone looked at Mr. James.

"Now that you own this place, what are you going to do to fix it up?" Debbie asked.

"That's a fair question, and that's why I'm here to find out what work needs to be done around here," Mr. James said.

"Well, you have already seen the busted front door. Half the steps in the front hallway are missing. The bells don't work," Vicky said.

"Those stairs are dangerous, and with my legs being in pain, I can't be jumping over them steps. I'm too old for all that, and the Mice..." Ms. Ruby added.

"Not just the mice, Ms. Ruby. Don't forget the roaches, and them silverfish bugs, too. Plus, the paint is all old and peeling." Debbie said.

"The water doesn't stay hot. I have to boil water in a pot to wash me and my son up," Janice said.

"And let's not forget these banisters," Debbie said.

Mr. James looked in amusement, "I hear you, ladies. I'll take care of all your complaints, starting today. I have my workers out front now, putting up a whole new door and building new stairs with good, sturdy wood. They won't be finished for another few days, so, I need you to keep using the back stairs, just a little while longer. I'd like to visit with each of you as well just to take a look at your apartments to see what needs to be fixed, so we can get started on the repairs soon," he assured.

"I'll make the appointment with the exterminator today and have them in here within the week. My workmen will check out the banisters and fix them up too. Now, ladies, all this won't happen overnight, but I promise, it will get done soon."

The ladies looked around in excitement talking to among One another.

CHAPTER ELEVEN

It was Sunday morning. Janice and Bobby sat on their porch with Bobby Jr. in his playpen. Ms. Ruby walked onto her porch using her cane.

"Good morning, Ms. Ruby!" Janice said.

"Morning, Janice! Would you and Bobby Jr. like to go to church with us this morning?"

Bobby lit up a cigarette. "We ain't church folks."

"I know you ain't, I didn't invite you. I'm talking to Janice. Or does she need your permission?"

"Look, I don't care about her going to worship a God that's never been there for her; a God that allowed her to become a part of the system; a God that gave her a crack-head mother. If she wants to waste her time going to a place like that, that's on her. I got some business to take care of." Bobby walked down the stairs and exited through the gate.

"That boy is hopeless. He doesn't care about anything but them streets. Satan got his mind and his tongue. That fast life will all come to an end, mark my words." Ms. Ruby said.

"He always tells me what to do, but never helps me do anything, including helping with Bobby, Jr. I mean, he doesn't do things with Bobby Jr. that a daddy should do with his son. He thinks giving me a few dollars for diapers is all there is to being a father;" Janice said.

"It takes a real man to raise a child, not the body parts they're bone with. As I told you before, you'll know when you're really tired."

"Tired?" Janice looked puzzled.

"Yes, tired," Ms. Ruby said.

"I am tired, Ms. Ruby. I just been scared of what Bobby may do if I try to leave, but you're right, Ms. Ruby, I'm going to see my Mommy."

"Do you remember that song?" "What song, Ms. Ruby?"

"Midnight Train to Georgia. You better ask Gladys Knight."

Janice disappeared into her apartment.

CHAPTER TWELVE

Debbie was grilling on her porch, getting ready for one of her card parties. Vicky sat on Debbie's porch.

Ms. Ruby walked out of her apartment supported by her cane and called up to the women.

"I smell barbecue!" Ms. Ruby said happily.

"Debbie's at it again, she's having a few people over." Vicky said. "Gambling, I bet. Lord, I remember them days," Ms. Ruby said.

Debbie walked to the steps looking down at Ms. Ruby with a spatula in one hand and a beer in the other. "You remember what days Ms. Ruby?"

"The card parties my girlfriends and I use to have back in the day. Our card games were keno, blackjack, and bridge. Child, I was young before, and trust me—I ain't always been Christian." Ms. Ruby wiggled as if dancing and the other women laughed.

"Vicky, I just buzzed your cousin in, he's coming up now," Willie said.

"Okay, Willie, tell him to come back here,".

Debbie's doorbell rang.

"Girl, everybody's showing up at the same time," Vicky added. "That's Gail! Buzz her in for me Vicky, while I flip this chicken." Vicky stepped into Debbie's apartment, as Jamie, Vicky's male cousin stepped out of Vicky's backdoor sporting a pair of black Diesel Jeans, black designer shoes, and a white Marc Jacob linen shirt holding a bottle of wine in his hand. Vicky exited Debbie's apartment and ran over to greet Jamie with a hug.

"Hey, Jamie!" Vicky yelled. "Hey, girl!"

"Sit your butt down over here! Looking flawless as always. Jamie, this is Debbie, my neighbor. She's the one throwing the card party."

"Hi there, Jamie, I hope you bought your coins!"

"Girl, I bought my coins and Pink Moscato." Jamie held up the bottle of wine.

"Well, we can drink that down too. I got some Belvidere if you want something a little stronger." Debbie stopped tending the grill long enough to pour some of her vodka into a red cup and handed it to Jamie.

"Vicky, I like your friend already!" Jamie said as he took a sip.

Gail stepped onto the porch from Debbie's apartment. "Everybody, this is my cousin, Gail!"

"Hey, everybody!" Gail said loudly.

"Oh, I didn't realize it's cousin's night! Gail, this is Jamie, my cousin from Indiana." Vcky said. Jamie and Gail both greeted each other as Gail took a seat at the table.

"Well, the food is ready now, let's get this party started!" Debbie said.

Hours had passed, and everyone was sitting at the table talking shit as they drank.

"I ain't had barbecue like this in a long time. Debbie, girl you need your own restaurant!" Jamie said.

"Yes, Debbie cooks her ass off!" Vicky said.

"Well, it's getting late… cuz, I'm about to head out," Gail said. "Me too! I'm going to call an Uber, ladies, and go spend a night at my BFF's house, but I need to use your bathroom first. I can't hold it any longer." Jamie said as he walked through Vicky's backdoor and quickly returned. "Vicky, Willie is in the bathroom blowing it up, can I use your bathroom, Debbie?"

"Do you have to do a number one or a number two?" Debbie said teasingly. "I'm just playing, you can use it." Debbie chuckled.

"Thank you!" Jamie said.

"And make sure to put the toilet seat down."

Debbie, Vicky, and Gail all began cleaning up their mess from the table.

Jamie exited Debbie's apartment with a shocked look on his face. "Wait one damn minute, what the hell is this?"

"Jamie, what's wrong with you? What are you doing with Debbie's picture?"

Jamie stared at the picture. "How the hell do you know Roscoe, Debbie?"

"Now, that's none of your business. Why the hell are you questioning me about my man? I don't talk to other hens about my man!" Jamie slammed the photo down on the table.

"No, this can't be the same Roscoe," Jamie said.

Gail sat down at the table. "Ummm…I don't think I'm leaving just yet, this look like it's about t be some real Jerry Springer shit." Gail was curious about what was happening.

"How long have you been seeing Roscoe?" Jamie was visibly upset. He was tearing up.

"You asking too many damn questions now, about my man!"

"Well, your so-called man, is my man too." Jamie pulled out his wallet and showed Debbie a picture of him and Roscoe hugged up. Vicky grabbed the wallet from Jamie. "Well, Roscoe must have a twin, because that's him in this picture, big nose and all."

Debbie snatched the wallet from Gail and looked closely at the photo. "I don't believe this shit!"

Gail lit up a joint. "I wasn't expecting a talk show but this here just got real."

"What you mean, he's your man, too?" Debbie grabbed the joint out of Gail's mouth and took a long puff.

"I must say this is a small world. Who would've thought my cousin and my friend were seeing the same man." Vicky said in a sad disbelieving tone.

"I've been seeing Roscoe for almost a year now. I met him in Indiana, at his cousin Jessie stepping party."

"Wow, so Roscoe been on the down-low."

"I should have suspected something when he only spends time with me on the weekends, but he also told me he couldn't stay during the week because he takes care of his mother."

"Roscoe's mother is dead! She died before I ever met Roscoe ass, and I been with his ass for three years." You could see the madness on Debbie's face.

Jamie sat down at the card table and placed his head in his hands.

"Look, I know it hurts to find out your man has been creeping.

Hell, I know from experience. There is no need for y'all to be upset with each other, but what y'all need to do is call his ass!" Gail added.

"Oh, I'm about to call his ass, all right." Debbie nodded in agreement.

"Damn, this is unreal," Vicky shaking her head in disbelief.

Jamie stood up, arms folded shaking his head back and forth. "Yeah, Gail, you're right!" Jamie fired up.

"Debbie, call that lying, cheating, bastard," Vicky said.

"Oh, I'm going to call him, and afterward, you can have him. You can take all his stuff with you too because I'm throwing the shit out of my house."

Gail walked into Debbie's apartment and returned with cups and vodka. She poured some into each cup and handed them to the others.

Debbie took a drink, then pulled out her phone, calling Roscoe. The phone rang several times before Roscoe answered.

"Hey, baby! Are you missing Big Daddy?" "Yes, Daddy, you know I am. When will you be home?" Debbie asked.

"I Should be back tomorrow morning. You make sure you're good and ready for Big Daddy," Roscoe said seductively.

"Oh, I'll be ready, Big Daddy, trust and believe that."

"So, how did the card party turn out?"

"Oh, it went really well. I meet some new players. Vicky's cousin from out of town even showed up."

"So how much did you win?"

"I won a whole lot of information."

"Information?! you ain't making no sense, baby. What Information are you talking about?"

Jamie shouted through the phone. "Oh, it's about to make a lot of sense, Roscoe."

"Who the hell is that? Debbie, you got some man over there?" "Yes, she got a man over here. The same man, you been sucking and fucking for the past year," Jamie said in the background, angrily.

"Who the hell is this?"

"You know who the hell this is!"

"Shit!!! How the hell...? It's not what y'all think, let me explain." Roscoe was shocked.

Everybody on the porch looked shocked.

"Your ass caught up now, Roscoe! I would have never thought you were on the down-low sleeping with the bro bro's." Debbie said angrily.

"Lying ass told me you were taking care of your mommy, but all this time it's been a woman. I can't say I'm mad, because she can cook her ass off," Jamie yelled into the phone.

All began to chuckle.

"You can say goodbye to all your shit. Your Jordans, your clothes, your video games. As a matter of fact, just don't even bother coming back here," Debbie said.

Gail and Vicky looked on as Debbie hung up the phone. "Look, Debbie, I'm so sorry, I didn't know."

"No need to apologize, I'm just glad I found out the truth. I mean, I ain't got nothing against gay men. Hell, I love them, especially my RuPaul. I just never thought it will be my man."

"Well, what did the piano man say in The Color Purple? Time to go," Gail said.

"It's not over just yet," Debbie said.

Everyone looked confused as Debbie ran into her apartment. She returned a moment later carrying clothes and shoes placing them on the grill.

"Debbie, you really going to burn the man clothes?!" Vicky asked.

"Girl, that's what the hell I should've done to Frank's stuff, burnt all his shit," Gail said.

"Debbie, sorry we had to meet like this, but I will say I enjoyed y'all's company."

"My uber pulling up, so I'll talk with you later, cuz." Then he said to Gail, "Nice meeting you, Gail."

"Yeah, I'm out of here, too. I'll talk to you later, Debbie."

CHAPTER THIRTEEN

It was the next morning. Bobby stood on his porch smoking while texting on his phone.

Scooter walked onto his porch, yawning, with a pill bottle in his hand.

"What's up, playa?"

"Oh, hey, Bobby!" Scooter rubbed his shoulder, then opened the pill bottle.

"What up Scooter, you popping pills now?"

"Nah, these pills help with the pain in my shoulder."

"Is your shoulder still bothering you? The way your grandma talks, her so-called God healed you already." Bobby said.

"I don't want to hear that God shit right now." Scooter tossed a pill in his mouth and swallowed. "Yeah, my shoulder still fucks with me. It hurts at times, but I can't let the coaching staff know.

If they knew the truth, my football career will be over before it starts."

"You'll be alright, remember, your Mr. MVP. Plus, you are working with a specialist, too."

"Yeah, the specialist helps. If it wasn't for him, I wouldn't be able to throw the ball; but on some real shit, I play that shit off, but my shoulder still be hurting. I can throw it, but not like I use to..." Scooter, looked disappointed, reopened the bottle, and pulled another pill out.

"So, how many of those do you take?"

"I take them when I need to. Once my shoulder is fully healed, I won't need them anymore."

"And your coach knows you're popping them like that?"

Scooter popped the pill into his mouth. "You think I'm going to show them I'm weak and still hurting?! Hell Nah! I got this!" Scooter said frustratedly.

"But you said you ain't throwing the ball like you use to." "Not like I was. I mean, I can still throw it and aim it but it's not 100%." Scooter sighed.

"Bruh, the pills might be your problem."

"Dude, you're a drug dealer, how the hell are you trying to talk to me about some pills?"

"You're right, I'm a drug dealer but I been in this game long enough to know when somebody is addicted. You addicted to the pills, Son..."

Ms. Ruby walked out onto her porch to join Scooter. "Morning, Scooter. Hello there, Bobby. So, what y'all two talking about?"

"Nothing, Grandma." Scooter looked at Bobby, who gave him a sly salute.

"I'm out! Remember what I said, Scooter." Scooter nodded. Bobby exited through the gate.

CHAPTER FOURTEEN

Several days had passed. Ms. Ruby sat on her porch sipping coffee as Janice walked onto her porch with an envelope in her hand leaning over the banister.

"Hi, Ms. Ruby! I see I got a letter from my school." Janice opened the envelope.

"So, what does the letter say child?"

Janice started to read the letter aloud, "We are pleased to inform you that you have successfully completed the nursing program!"

"That's great, Janice! Didn't I say God would get you through," Ms. Ruby said.

"Ms. Ruby, I can do that internship now!" Janice said joyfully.

Janice kissed the paper. "I can't wait to tell my mommy." "So, how did that ever go, meeting your mommy?"

Janice walked over to Ms. Ruby's porch and took a seat. "It's been wonderful. I have seen her twice already. We've been talking on the phone every day Ms. Ruby. I wish you could've seen her with Bobby Jr. She wouldn't let him go!" Janice looked around conspiratorially." "She asked me to move in with her. She and her husband have a four-bedroom house and her husband is a minister, and he has a daughter, too, around my age. She's in school, studying to become a lawyer.

"Look, you finished your program. You are developing a relationship with your mother now and she even asked you to move in with her. Child, I think you are finally getting through that storm. So, are you going to move in with her and her husband?" Ms. Ruby asked.

"I think so. It's such a good opportunity. I can focus on my internship and finding myself a good job."

"See! Now you're talking that grown women talk." Ms. Ruby said.

Bobby walked onto the porch and dropped his duffel bag on one of the chairs. "Janice, what the hell you doing? Can't you hear Bobby Jr. crying?"

"I'm coming! I just needed to talk to Ms. Ruby real quick. You know, he's your son, too."

"Yeah, but I got some business to take care of. I don't have time to be babysitting."

"It's not babysitting when it's your child." Ms. Ruby replied.

Bobby gave Ms. Ruby a dirty look. "Ms. Ruby, my business is my business, whether it's street or not. You need to worry about what's going on in your own home with your grandson instead of worrying about what's going on over here."

"Now Janice, go get Bobby Jr."

"Son, you talk to her like she's a child. She's a grown woman and your son's mother. You need to talk to her with some respect."

"There you go again, all up in our business. You need to worry about your grandson and stop being all up in other folks' business." Bobby pulled out his phone and begin to scroll through it. Janice stood up, sighed, and walked toward Bobby.

"Bobby, she's right. You treat me like trash, and I've had enough. I'm leaving! I'm taking Bobby Jr. and we're moving in with my mom." Janice was speaking with newfound confidence.

Bobby was shocked by Janice unexpectedly standing up to him. "What the hell you say Bitch?!" Bobby grabbed Janice violently by the arm. "You're not taking my son to live with that dope fiend mommy of yours."

Janice pulled her arm away from Bobby forcefully. She again spoke with confidence. "Bobby, she's not on drugs anymore, I saw her, and she's clean. It's not up to you what me and my child going to do. You don't take care of him anyways. You have never been a father to Bobby Jr. You been a daddy to them streets though. We don't need you; we're leaving."

Bobby was getting increasingly angry. "Oh, you think your wonder women now? Listening to this old lady is going to get your ass beat!"

Bobby balled up his fists and jumped towards Janice. Ms. Ruby grabbed her broom and rushed towards Bobby swinging the broom at him. "Boy, if you even think about hitting her, this broom will split your head!" Ms. Ruby said sternly.

Willie and Vicky heard the commotion and rushed down the stairs. Willie was confused, trying to make sense of the commotion. "What's going on down here?!"

Vicky hurried to Ms. Ruby's side, visibly nervous. "Ms. Ruby are you okay?!"

"This boy is trying to jump on Janice because she told him she's finally leaving him!"

Willie stepped between Bobby and Janice.

"I can't let you do that, Bob!" Willie said.

Bobby got up in Willie's face. "This ain't what you want, Willie.

This is between me and my baby mommy."

"It's between all of us when it comes to you putting your hands on a woman," Willie said calmly, but very firmly.

There was a silent moment of tension, then Bobby and Janice's doorbell rings. Janice walked into the apartment. Bobby tried to follow her, but Willie stopped him. "Who the hell ringing our bell, Bobby said with a frown on his face?"

Janice walked back out onto the porch carrying Bobby Jr. She was followed by two police detectives, Detective Carter and Detective Grant.

These detectives are looking for Bobby. Bobby grabbed his duffel bag and started heading down the stairs.

"Bobby Johnson, stop right there! Put your hands up." Detective Carter said.

"What the hell do y'all want with me?!" Bobby stopped, dropping his bag as the detectives approached him.

"You are wanted in connection with the murder of Shawn Jenkins, and the attempted murders of Bobby Johnson Jr. and Calvin Walker." Detective Grant handcuffed Bobby.

"Murder?! I didn't murder nobody, and then you're saying I tried to murder my own son? Now, why in the hell would I do that? I think y'all got the wrong Bobby Johnson." Bobby trying to resist arrest.

"Wait, did you say Calvin Walker? That's my Scooter!" Ms. Ruby said in disbelief.

"Grant, grab Bobby's bag. Let's see why Mr. Johnson was in such a hurry to leave with it."

Detective Grant opened the bag and pulled out a brick of marijuana, baggies of heroin, and handguns.

"Look at what we got here." Detective Grant said. He continued rifling through the bag emptying its contents.

"Wait, I'm confused! Detectives, what are you saying? Bobby killed somebody, and shoot my son, and Scooter?" Janice asked.

She then passed Bobby Jr. to Vicky and walked down the stairs towards Bobby.

"Are my ears deceiving me?! Bobby was the one who shot my Scooter?" Ms. Ruby was frustrated and growing increasingly anxious. She tried to rush down the stairs too, but stopped and clutched her chest in emotional pain. "He tried to kill my grandson?!" Ms. Ruby was screaming.

Debbie stepped on the porch. "What the hell is going on down there?!" Debbie walked down the stairs.

"These detectives said Bobby was the one who shot my Scooter, and his own baby, and killed that other man." Ms. Ruby was in shock.

"Janice, this is crazy! I didn't kill anybody. I don't know what the hell they are talking about." Bobby looked over his shoulder to address the detectives. "You got the wrong guy!"

"That's what they all say when they get caught. Do you know a Donta Harris?" Bobby looked confused.

"No, I don't know anybody named Donta."

"Okay, let me rephrase that. Do you know a Jo-Jo?"

"I know a Jo-Jo, but I don't fuck with him like that. My name Bobby, not Jo-Jo. You got the wrong dude."

"Ahh, so you do know him," Detective Carter said.

"Do you remember selling him a gun?"

Bobby shook his head slowly. "I don't know what you're talking about."

"You sold a nine-millimeter handgun to Donta aka Jo-Jo. The same nine-millimeter handgun that was used in the drive-by shooting at the pizza bowl that killed a man and injured your own son, and Calvin Walker."

"Man, I ain't saying nothing. I want a lawyer."

"Bobby, you have the right to remain silent. Anything you say can be—"

Bobby interrupted, "Yeah Yeah, I heard it all before."

Janice was in surprised shock. "Bobby, what did you do?! What did you do?!" Janice slapped Bobby across the face, then began beating him in the chest. "That gun nearly killed our son!"

"I didn't know!" Bobby fell to his knees crying but was pulled up by Detective Carter. "I didn't know!"

"Boy, you lucky I'm too old to run down there! I'd slap you, too. Ms. Ruby said as she breathed heavily.

I told you, living that fast life will get you in one or two places, dead, or in jail. Now, look where you are headed!" Ms. Ruby yelled.

Debbie rubbed Ms. Ruby's back as she sat in the chair. Ms. Ruby shook her head as tears fell down her face.

"It's going to be okay, Ms. Ruby. It's going to be okay." Debbie continued to rub Ms. Ruby's back to comfort her.

Janice walked up the steps and retrieves Bobby Jr. from Vicky.

Janice was joyful still trying to come to terms with all that's happened. "The chain has been broken. We're free, Bobby, Jr, we're free. I will never let anyone ever hurt you again." Janice began to sob, overcome with emotions.

CHAPTER FIFTEEN

It's in the afternoon, a few days later. Coach Johnson called Ms. Ruby. "Hi Ms. Ruby, I need to talk to you. I believe Scooter has a problem that needs to be addressed."

"A problem, Coach? What type of problem?"

"I believe he's been overmedicating with painkillers. Have you noticed any changes in his attitude?"

"You mean he's been popping pills? Lord, why haven't I noticed?! I've been too worried about my own health!"

"It's not your fault, Ms. Ruby. An injury like Scooters which he has sustained can have people taking more than what's prescribed, which can lead to addiction."

"Scooter, not no addict coach, he's a ballplayer. A good kid. "This has nothing to do with him as a person, but it does have something to do with the pain he's been hiding.

"If you want to point the blame, I'll take responsibility. I knew he was pushing himself hard, but I didn't know it would lead to this. I found a program that Scooter can attend that will help him get off the pills and back on the field. With your permission, I can get him in."

"So, you think this program will help him get off those pills?"

"I think it's a start, and the rest will be up to Scooter."

"Will he still be able to play football, coach? Once he completes this program? That's all he talks about doing."

"We can't worry about that right now. Our main goal is to give him our support, no matter what."

"Of course, coach. You're right. I'll do whatever I need to support him."

"I'll call now to make arrangements to get Scooter in the program, in the meantime, be easy with him. I'll talk to you later, Ms. Ruby."

Coach Johnson hung up and Ms. Ruby picked up her Bible from the table, looked at it, then tossed it to the ground.

"Lord, all I ask is, why? I then done everything you asked of me. I help out my community. I pay my tithes. I'm good to people. I became a good Christian," Ms. Ruby was crying out in emotional pain. "Why Lord? Why my grandson? Lord, he's all I got. Please, Lord, I ask that you take his pain away. Give him the strength Lord to overcome this addiction.

"But, not only him, please give me strength lord, to get Scooter through this. The devil comes hitting hard, and I ask that you be my coach, and teach me to swing back harder." Ms. Ruby fell to her knees, holding her cane, tearing up. Ms. Ruby said faintly, "He's all I got Lord."

Weeks later, the building is significantly improved. Ms. Ruby sat on her porch sipping her coffee, looking through her lottery tickets while Debbie sat on her porch playing solitaire at the table, smoking a cigarette. Willie walked onto his porch in a baseball uniform with a bat in hand.

"What a beautiful morning. I say, what a beautiful morning it is." Willie took the bat, hitting the side of one of his cleats.

"Willie, why you over there looking like a wannabe, Willie Mays?" Debbie asked.

"Ain't no wannabe over here. I put the balls past the wall." Willie posed as if he were hitting a baseball.

"Now, I know it's not Halloween yet, so why in the hell are you dressed like that?" Debbie asked again.

"Real funny, Debbie, real funny. But since you asked, it's our annual building picnic softball game. You didn't know I grow up in the Robert Taylor's 45th and State, baby! 45th and State."

"That sounds like fun. Is there going to be any single men out there? Preferably working straight ones." Debbie asked.

Vicky walked onto the porch and handed Willie a cup of coffee. "I see you out here, running your mouth." Vicky kissed Willie on the cheek.

"Nah baby, but I'm about to show up and show out." Willie began to swing the bat.

"Mmm Hmm! Okay, baby, and I made sure I put the hot and cold cream in your bag too."

"Hey there, Vicky." Ms. Ruby said.

"Hey there, Ms. Ruby!" Vicky walked down to Ms. Ruby's porch and sat next to her.

"Why is your husband dressed up like Ernie Banks?" Ms. Ruby asked.

"Debbie said Willie Mays, and you say, Ernie Banks."

Vicky giggled, "He's playing in some softball game today for the building he grew up in as a child."

Willie joined Vicky and Ms. Ruby on Ms. Ruby's porch. "Hey, Ms. Ruby! I heard the good news. You must be very excited."

"What news?" Ms. Ruby put down her lottery tickets, looking up at Willie.

"The news about Scooter."

"Oh, Lord, what news?" Ms. Ruby said nervously.

"Now, don't go getting upset, Ms. Ruby. It's nothing bad." Willie reassured her.

Ms. Ruby looked at Vicky confused, "Don't look at me, I don't know what he's talking about."

"I knew that grandson of yours would make it. The boy has always been gifted and strong. UIC gave Scooter the scholarship, full- ride in all!"

Debbie walked down the stairs to join the others. "What's this I hear about Scooter?!"

"Willie said he saw on TV that UIC give Scooter the scholarship to play football there." Ms. Ruby said proudly.

"Shout your mouth! That's great! He deserves it, especially since all the stuff he's been going through." Debbie said.

"Let me wake the boy up and tell him the good news." Ms. Ruby stood with her cane and hollered through the screen door.

"Scooter get out here, I got some news for your ears." Ms. Ruby yelling with excitement in her voice.

Scooter stepped out onto the porch stretching, rubbing his eyes. "Yes, grandma, what is it?!"

"You got the scholarship, UIC gave you the scholarship!"

"Are you serious, Grandma!?! How do you know? Did coach call?"

"It was just on the news, UIC said they were giving you a full scholarship!"

"I got the scholarship! I got the scholarship!" Scooter was emotional and tearful. He looked at his phone. "I see I have missed calls from the coach, let me go call him!" Scooter ran into the house, excitedly.

"I told that boy, a little mustard seed of faith is all he needed. He got through the therapy, the rehab and now the Lord then gave him a chance to play football again." Ms. Ruby was smiling as she sat back in her chair, leaning on her cane, shaking her head in happily.

"That's great, Ms. Ruby! I'm happy for Scooter. Now, I'm about to take Willie to his softball game, is there anything you need me to do before I leave?" Vicky asked.

"I do want to check these old lottery tickets I found in my drawer from months ago, but I could wait for you to check them later."

Vicky grabbed Ms. Ruby's phone.

"What are you doing child? Is there a number you can call to check the tickets?

Vicky scrolled through Ms. Ruby's phone. "No, Ms. Ruby! There's an app you can use that will show you the winning lottery numbers. I'm downloading it now for you."

"An app? All I use that phone for is to make calls and listen to my gospel music, and Scooter set that up for me. So, it's just that easy? Can you check these two "pick threes" for me? I think I got a mega, too.

"App downloaded, let me check." Vicky scanned the lottery tickets with Ms. Ruby's phone.

"Sorry, Ms. Ruby, these two are not winners."

There was a brief moment of silence. In a surprising tone, she said, "Wait wait, wait, are my eyes deceiving me?!"

Vicky took a close look at the phone and ticket at the same time, with a big smile on her face. Willie tried to grab the phone from Vicky, but she swatted his hand away.

"Vicky, it's not nice to have an old lady waiting. Now, what is it, child?"

Vicky leaned over to show Ms. Ruby the screen.

Debbie's curiosity was overtaking her. She spoke impatiently. "Vicky, I'm like Ms. Ruby, what the damn ticket say?"

"Whoa. Whoa, Whoa,! Ms. Ruby, you hit five out of six numbers—Ms. Ruby, do you hear me?!"

"You hit five out of six numbers!" Vicky Joyfully shouted.

"THAT'S A MILLION DOLLARS MS. RUBY!! A MILLION DOLLARS."

"Child, stop playing! Did I hear you right?" Ms. Ruby looked over the numbers on her phone and seeing the whole thing was not a joke, she grinned from ear to ear, stood up, and began sliding across the porch, like James Brown.

"That's a double whammy, Ms. Ruby! Scooter getting a scholarship, and us winning 1,000,000 dollars," Debbie added on.

Scooter walked out onto the porch over to the group.

"Grandma, what's going on?"

"Your grandma had me check some old lottery tickets and she hit for one million dollars Scooter. One million," Vicky said.

Scooter and Vicky interlocked arms and began singing, "we're moving on up"

"Speaking of moving on up, don't the good book say it's better to give than to-," Debbie said.

Ms. Ruby smiling, shaking her head at Debbie. "I already know where this is going. To tell you the truth, you and Vicky remind me of Scooter's mother. I love you both like you were my own daughters. Now, first things first. I need to sign the back of this ticket. Second, I need to call my lawyer, so we can get the ball rolling.

And third, I will be writing you two checks in the amount of $25,000."

Vicky clapped her hands together, in awe, "Ms. Ruby!"

Debbie was also in awe, "Pinch me, I must be dreaming!"

Ms. Ruby pinched Debbie's arm, and Debbie screamed out.

"Are you dreaming?" Ms. Ruby asked.

"Oh, thank you, Ms. Ruby! Now, I can get that food truck I have always been wanting," Debbie said.

"Yes, thank you, Ms. Ruby! Willie and I can make a down payment on a house with $25,000 dollars!" Vicky added.

"Yes, and once we have a house, we can adopt ourselves a baby boyyyyyy," Willie shouted.

Vicky swatted at Willie, and punched him in the arm, playfully. "What about a girl?" "I don't care, boy or girl. Thanks again, Ms. Ruby!" Willie hugged Ms. Ruby, picking her up off her feet.

"The Lord has blessed me, and I want to share that blessing with the people I love." Ms. Ruby stood on her newly energized legs and raised her arms singing, "Never Could've Made It Without You" with the others singing along."

"Thank you, Lord, for your blessings, and those to come," Ms. Ruby said.

THE END

www.ingramcontent.com/pod-product-compliance
Lightning Source LLC
Chambersburg PA
CBHW071224170626
46809CB00005BA/1929